A HELLEQUIN N

INFAMOUS
REIGN

STEVE McHUGH

INFAMOUS REIGN

A Hellequin Novella

Steve McHugh

*For everyone who supported me when I was an unknown self-published writer,
and for everyone who continues to do so.
Thank you.*

ALSO BY STEVE MCHUGH

The Hellequin Chronicles

Crimes Against Magic

Born of Hatred

With Silent Screams

Prison of Hope

Lies Ripped Open

Promise of Wrath

Scorched Shadows

Infamous Reign

Frozen Rage

The Avalon Chronicles

A Glimmer of Hope

A Flicker of Steel

A Thunder of War

Hunted

The Rebellion Chronicles

Sorcery Reborn

Death Unleashed

Horsemen's War

Stand Alone

Blackcoat

CHAPTER 1

September 1483, Tower of London.

It's surprisingly easy to gain access to a king when many of his most trusted servants and advisers also work for you.

The king's guard all moved aside, most ensuring they didn't make eye contact. Those who knew who I was also had a pretty good idea of why I was there, and so avoided me for that reason. Those who didn't know me must have sensed my dark mood and decided that pissing me off further than I already seemed to be wouldn't have enhanced their chances for a quiet life.

Thus unencumbered, I made my way through the courtyard of the royal palace toward the Grand Hall, where the king was holding court. I reached the doors and opened them, stepping through into a room that lived up to its name.

The hall was both massive and opulent, with the king's banners showing the House of York's white rose, alongside the usual imagery of fleur-de-lis and inaccurate looking griffins draped next to stunning stained glass windows, some of which depicted the king's personal badge, a white boar.

Several dozen men and women, of all ages and ranks, stood before King Richard III of England as he sat on his throne. Each subject was given the opportunity, in turn, to ask or beg the king for whatever favor he or she wished. Some wishes were granted, some were not, it was wholly dependent on the king's mood of the day and how much he either liked or needed the petitioner. The king's judgment was final, too. Sometimes you got a good king, a just king, a king who would help his people. And sometimes you got a blood-thirsty savage. Either way, so long as Merlin and Avalon were happy, we didn't intervene in human politics. Unfortunately, on this day, Merlin was far from happy. Which led to the reason why I was here.

I resisted the temptation to make a point by removing anyone but the king from the room. He was finishing up a proclamation that permitted one of his subjects to marry someone else, and I allowed the moment to continue. It wasn't them I was angry with.

When the king finished, he noticed me for the first time, and all color drained from his face. If you're the ruler of a country and I'm standing before you, it's usually not because you're doing a good job. The first time it happens is just after a coronation. I, or someone just like me, arrives and tells you exactly where you stand in the world and explain that you either behave, which means doing the things we ask, or you'll receive another, less pleasant, visit.

The king before me knew exactly why I was there. Two princes, Edward and Richard, had vanished after being placed in his custody. He was either personally involved in something very bad, or he knew who was. It had been left for me to either fix it or to ensure that it was King Richard III's final error.

King Richard signaled to one of his aides who then told everyone that court was over and would reconvene on the morrow. I stood still as the confused masses were ushered from the hall, until only the king and I were left.

"I know why you're here," he said.

"That should make this go a lot quicker then," I snapped and walked toward him. "Your majesty." I didn't bow or even nod in his direction. That wasn't a judgment against the man; there wasn't a human king or queen alive that I would have done it for. None of them were *my* king.

"Hellequin, you have to understand." Fear broke through his voice.

I stopped walking and ignited a ball of fire in the palm of my hand, making it turn slowly. "Make me understand, Richard," I said softly. "Make me realize why you disobeyed an order from Merlin."

King Richard III of England was not a small man. In fact in many quarters he would have been described as formidable, both in stature and presence, but he appeared visibly uncomfortable at the sight of the flames moving over my palm.

"I've done nothing to make Merlin unhappy," he told me firmly.

I walked over to the nearest window and looked out at the courtyard. Several lords and ladies of court were chatting amongst themselves, while a large black canine leaned up against a nearby wall, in the shade. He glanced my way briefly, as if aware that I was looking down on him.

I turned back to look at the King. He wasn't a young man by human standards, having nearly turned thirty, but he still had several decades ahead of him, barring illness or war. Unfortunately, crossing Avalon was going to shorten his lifespan.

"I have done nothing to upset Merlin," Richard repeated, a slight desperation in his voice. "He has no reason to send you here."

"I gave you those boys to look after," I said softly, struggling to control the anger that bubbled inside.

"I don't understand."

"The princes are important. I removed them from the Woodville's, who would only have used them for their own ends, and I gave them to you—a man I thought I could trust to take care of the young king and his brother. I instructed you to keep them safe, to have them cast as illegitimate children, after which I would return to collect them. I remember telling you this using only small words, so you'd understand its importance."

"I did as you asked. I had them renounced, and I took over as King. What more did you want from me?"

"Where are they?" my voice was cold and hard.

Richard's eyes avoided my gaze.

"Do I need to repeat myself?"

"I do not know where they are," he whispered.

"You don't know?" I shouted, slamming my hand onto the nearby table, making Richard recoil slightly. "How do you fucking-well lose two princes?"

A fire of defiance lit in his eyes. "You will do well to remember that *I* am king here, *Hellequin*."

A blast of air magic threw Richard from his feet and pinned him against the far wall as I stalked toward him.

"And you would do well to watch your tongue, lest I remove it along with your head."

I released the magic, and he crashed to the ground, yelling out in pain. I'd forgotten about his twisted back, a well-hidden deformity hardly anyone knew. But the constant pain occasionally made its way through the mask of normality. A twinge of guilt went through me. I pushed the thought aside. I had a job to do. It was more important that the kings of the land understand their place, than it was that I felt good about my actions.

I offered the king my hand. He refused and pushed himself off the floor, anger in his eyes.

"Do you know why you're king?" I asked.

"Because you needed someone to take over," he snapped. "Someone you could threaten and use."

I shook my head. "Merlin could have picked anyone for that. *I* picked you because I like you. You're a good man; ruthless, smart and above all, capable of being a good king. Someone your subjects can look up to and admire. But right now, you're the king who murders children in a tower." The fact that Richard had been my choice for king was another reason I was so angry. Merlin had declared the issue to be my problem to deal with above all others. I didn't like to be made to look stupid.

"They're not dead."

"Does that matter? The story is out there, and it will build and gain momentum until the only thing people remember about Richard the Third is you had to murder children to become king."

"I told you, I didn't murder them. I haven't harmed them in any way. I don't understand why are they so important to you."

"That isn't your concern. Now, you have no idea of the trouble it causes me to come to London. So, for the final time, you *will* tell me where they are."

"Those boys are my blood and therefore my concern—no matter what you or anyone else from Avalon wishes to believe. I had them removed from the tower. I told trusted men to take them north of here, away from London. They're not safe in the city, not even in the tower."

"Really? Then please do tell me what you thought was going to happen here."

"There has been talk of people who wish to kill them and use their murders against me. This country doesn't need more war. We need stability."

"So they were removed from the city because that's what was safe for you?"

"For everyone."

Despite the fact that Richard was clearly outmatched, he still exuded confidence. He was certain that his decision to remove the princes from the tower was the best choice available to him.

"Whom did you send them with?"

"The Duke of Buckingham, he's taken the boys to Wales."

"And may I ask why you didn't think it important to inform Avalon of your plans?"

"Buckingham sent a messenger to you."

If nothing else, I had to admire the conviction of his belief in those who worked for him. Even if it was misplaced. "I think we can safely say that didn't happen. Or that the messenger was intercepted."

Panic crossed his face. "They left only a few days ago, but I had the boys confined to their quarters for the past month before then. Something is happening and I don't wish for them to be involved."

I sighed, disappointed that Richard had done nothing to get Avalon's help, making a bad situation worse. "I'll go after them. In the future, when Avalon tells you to do something, you do it. Because, I assure you that I will be far and away the least of your worries if anything has happened to those princes."

"And Hellequin, you should remember, that they are my nephews. And if Avalon's plans for them fall into anything that harms them, I will seek retribution for it."

I couldn't help but respect the fact that even though Richard knew Avalon could remove him from power at Merlin's whim, he still stood up for what he believed in. "Merlin's plans will keep them safe, I promise."

"Merlin is not here."

"*I'll* keep them safe, Richard. But first I have to find them.

In the meantime, you'd best pray that when I reach them, they're still in one piece." I truly hoped that the power of his kingship wouldn't change Richard, as it had so many before him. I didn't want to make a third, much less pleasant, nighttime visit.

CHAPTER 2

The courtyard had gotten busier and busier since my arrival. With the king having ended his court so abruptly, many of those who had wished to see him, were still milling around hoping their liege would change his mind.

The large canine I'd spotted earlier had vanished, so I made my way toward the stables where I found a young man leaning against a tree trunk. He was roughly the same height as I, but even more broad across the shoulders. When we'd first met, he'd been an English archer and the only survivor of an attack on the city of Soissons by a pack of vicious werewolves. They'd managed to replace his humanity with the beast that resided inside him, but did not break him as they'd hoped. Despite the lack of the middle and fourth fingers on his right hand, Thomas still practiced with a war bow every day. For a while he'd tried to teach me the subtle uses of the deadly weapon. But, while I was strong enough to pull the bow and accurate enough to hit my target, Thomas's mastery made me look like a child with a new toy. He was fluid and graceful, and his new werewolf speed and strength had made him even more dangerous.

"I thought you always spooked the horses," I commented as we shook hands.

"I've been learning to control it. I don't think I'll ever be able to ride one, but then I didn't before Soissons either, so that's not really a huge loss." He grinned. "How are you Nathaniel?"

"I'm good, thanks, Thomas." As much as I'd liked to have gone for a drink to catch up on his progress within Avalon, not to mention his evolving abilities, such pleasantries would have to wait until the current crisis was resolved. Thomas had been a werewolf for nearly seventy years. But that was nothing in terms of their life expectancy, and every time I'd seen him since his turning, I'd been surprised at new things he'd picked up. "I noticed you lounging in the courtyard when I glanced out of the Grand Hall's window. Does anyone ever get curious about a large, black wolf roaming the castle?"

"Oddly, no. A few of the guests have brought wolves with them as pets. Besides, very few people in the city of London would even know what a real wolf looked like."

"So, how has your time here treated you?"

"I never realized just how much gossip people discuss when they think there's no one around to hear it. The filth that goes on in that place." He waved dramatically to include the entire castle beside us. "It's a surprise anyone ever gets anything done with all the bed hopping and attempted seduction that goes on."

"And did any of that gossip manage to contain something useful?" I asked.

"All gossip is useful to the right person."

I chuckled. "You've spent far too much time with the SOA." The SOA, or Shield of Avalon, was Avalon's internal security force. They were considered masters of subversion and information gathering, all in the name of keeping Avalon and its citizens safe. Or learning as much about those in positions of power around the world, including Avalon itself, to use for their own ends. It all depended on whom you asked.

"I guess my purpose here has ended. I assume you want me

to go back to Avalon and report?"

I shook my head. "Did you get my note? I sent it a few weeks ago, after I'd learned about the princes'."

Thomas nodded. "You wanted me to start looking around to find out if anyone was planning anything against either the boys or the king. A lot of people here think Richard had them killed, or maybe Henry reached out from France to frame him. That's quite a popular theory, too. Some people change their minds on the subject, depending on whom they're talking to at the time."

"Any of them stand out?"

"One does. He was nobody before Richard took the throne, but recently he started to drop some very big names as friends. Buckingham being one of them."

"What's his name?"

"William Tate. He's a weasel of a man, even by the lords of London's quite low standards. I've caught wind of something he's involved in, but I'm not exactly sure of the details, something to do with jewels. He sent his wife and son away the day the two princes stopped appearing in public. He's currently having his way with a maid and likes to talk far too much after he's finished."

"Please don't tell me you had to—"

"Thankfully, no. The maid also likes to talk to a large, black dog that roams the grounds. She finds him adorable."

"I'm beginning to think the truth of it is that this dog finds *himself* adorable," I said with a smile. One that Thomas returned.

"You're just jealous."

"So, where does this William Tate live?"

"I'll take you, it isn't far. Maybe an hour or so."

"No, meet me there by dusk. I need you to bring someone with you."

"Okay, who?"

"Are there any changelings in the city?"

Thomas's smile broadened. "Master Garrett, you, sir, have a devious mind."

"Says Mr. Carpenter, the spy for Avalon."

"I never said I disapproved," Thomas said with a laugh. He then gave me directions to William Tate's house and set off on the errand I'd given him.

Once Thomas had left, I found my horse and was soon riding through the streets of London. It wasn't a pastime I enjoyed, although the fact that it was still daylight meant that at least no one tried to attack me. Unfortunately, it also meant that I could see the state of the city itself. Rats, some huge and vicious, ran freely through the streets spreading disease among the vast number of people who lived and worked here. The plague had eradicated a substantial number of the city's inhabitants over a hundred years ago, and, although London was, once again, a rapidly growing city, the threat of the plague's re-emergence was always a concern.

However, the growing number of humans, all with their own needs and desires, meant there was money to be made. And living amongst them were people who would profit from their misery. No matter what else happened in London, no matter the war and death, there was always one constant; there would be those who profited.

Despite the danger that the nighttime in London brought with it, I wasn't concerned about my friend Thomas living there. I doubted there'd be any trouble he couldn't take care of. In fact, if he did have trouble, there would probably be less pick-pockets or thugs to prey on the rest of the city.

CHAPTER 3

Lord Tate's property sat at the far end of the wealthy district in London, a place where the streets were maintained regularly and the owners all had at least two servants. I led the horse to the front door, where another horse was hitched, and climbed down, just as the door opened and a haggard-looking man rushed out.

"Lord Tate?" I questioned, as he hastily attached a bag to the horse's saddle.

"I don't know who you are, but I'm a very busy man, so please leave at once."

I walked toward the clearly nervous man. "I'm not here for fun, Lord Tate. We need to talk about Buckingham and the two princes."

His already pasty skin whitened further. "I don't know what you're talking about," he managed to stammer.

"There are a plethora of lies you could have told me about your involvement, but everyone in the country knows about those two boys, so unless you're currently living under a rock, maybe you'd like to try again."

"I told you to leave," he snapped.

"Last chance."

Lord Tate whirled on me. "I said—"

I hit him in the stomach hard enough to bring him to his knees as he fought for the breath that had fled his body. I removed the bag from his saddle and carried both it and Lord Tate back into his house.

I'd expected many things from his living space, most especially opulence and grandeur of the kind you get from people who like to pretend they're more powerful and influential then they really are. Maybe even a few stuffed animals that he would brag about while throwing overly lavish parties, telling his guests that he'd killed them with his bare hands.

What I didn't expect were a dead maid and butler.

The latter was leaning up against the far wall, opposite the front door. He appeared to have just sat down, except for blood soaking through the front of his clothes. The maid was just visible in the hallway. She'd been stabbed repeatedly; her entire body was covered in blood, as were the floor and walls all around her.

I saw all of this before I'd even closed the front door and dropped the bag on the floor. I threw Lord Tate into the hallway, where he landed in the pool of blood surrounding the murdered maid's body. He quickly scrambled away, as if it were the first time he'd seen her.

"Are you frightened of your own handiwork?" I enquired, picking the bag up and walking toward a room at the rear of the house, the open door showing it to be a study. Tate tried to scamper away, but I used a little wind magic, wrapping it around his leg, making sure he couldn't buck or twist free as I dragged him behind me. I dropped him by his desk before pushing the piles of paperwork and books that adorned the top of the desk onto the floor with an almighty crash.

"When I upend this bag onto your desk, what am I going to find?"

"Nothing of your concern," he said far too quickly.

"I swear, if this is what I think it is I'm going to be very angry." I placed one foot on his knee and pushed down, causing him to yell out. "And an angry me, would be very bad for your life expectancy."

The bag did not contain what I assumed it would. I was expecting correspondence between Tate and King Richard's enemies. Maybe some money or jewels that could be used to buy their support after Tate fled the city. But what clattered onto the wooden desk top were the two crowns, the smaller spinning slightly before I stopped it with my hand.

"Tate. Why are there two crowns in your bag?" I lifted the smaller crown, a plain gold piece that would have been used for a young prince. The second, and larger, one had red velvet covering the centre. There were very few jewels on the crown, certainly nowhere near the number that adorned the crown of the current king of England.

"You cannot touch them," he said. "They cannot be sullied by your hand."

He moved to take them from the table, but I kicked him back to the floor. "Tate, I've been looking for a way to use some of this anger that's been building up inside me since I arrived in London. For your sake, you really don't want to be the person I decide to take out my annoyance out on. So I'll ask again. What and who are these crowns for?"

I already knew the answer to my question, but I wanted it confirmed. I knew once the words left his lips I would kill him right there and then. I was begging for an excuse to put the sniveling little shit out of his misery. Unfortunately, Tate remained silent.

The momentary respite gained by his silence was just enough for me to calm down to a point where I wasn't going to kill him outright. Instead, I grabbed him from the floor and threw him roughly into the chair on the opposite side of the table. "These are for Edward and his brother, yes?"

Tate nodded. "Richard's crown is tainted. We need a new crown for the true king. The prince's should match it in design."

"You were taking these to Buckingham."

He nodded again.

"He has the boys?"

Another nod.

"Where is he?"

This time Tate just stared at the crowns and didn't move.

"Tate, where is Buckingham?"

"Richard is an impostor. Edward is our rightful king. I am doing the right thing for this country."

"Really? Why kill the butler and maid?"

He actually had the decency to look ashamed. "The maid and I were having an affair."

"Are you going to tell me her name?"

Tate shook his head again. "You don't need to know it."

I accepted his desire to keep it to himself. "So, why kill her?"

"She found out about the crowns and was going to tell people she knew at court. We would have been stopped. So she had to be silenced."

"And the butler?"

"He wasn't meant to be here today. He was upstairs when I killed her, and he surprised me. Then he died too." His words were said softly, the shock of what he'd done was beginning to set in, but I couldn't let that shock get in the way of the answers I needed.

"So, where are Buckingham and the boys?" I asked, hoping to

get his attention onto more immediate matters.

"I won't tell you."

I removed a small silver dagger from the rear of my belt and laid it on the desk. "Yes, Tate, you will."

"You won't stop them. Our rightful king will be placed on the throne of England."

I shook my head. "You're either naive or stupid. The princes will be taken to France, assuming they're still alive, and Henry will use their names to come over here and fight Richard. At some point, there will be a terrible accident and the boys will die, leaving Henry to be king. The boys are just being used to further Buckingham and his allies' aims. They will no more sit on the throne of England, than I will."

Tate didn't want to believe me. He was clearly desperate to believe that he was helping Edward and his brother, but my words had triggered the one dangerous thing in a mind that's been made-up, doubt. Tate had probably never before considered the scenario I'd painted for him, but the second he let that possibility in, it began to fester. Unfortunately, I didn't have time for Tate to decide whether or not he wanted to help.

I grasped his hand and forced it onto the table as I picked up the dagger. I was about to plunge it through his hand, when the front door opened. "Nathaniel," Thomas called out.

"We're back here," I told him and released the lord's hand.

A moment later Thomas and a second man entered the room. The newcomer was tall and thin, with an almost bald head and a short, dark beard, which had been meticulously trimmed. There was nothing about him that would call attention to the fact that he was anything other than human.

"This is Raulf," Thomas said. "Raulf, this is Nathaniel."

"A pleasure to meet you, my lord," Raulf said, and we shook hands.

"Nathaniel will do, I'm no one's lord." I turned back to Tate. "However, this murderous bastard *is* a lord, although not for very long."

"Why are they here?" Tate demanded. "I don't care how many you bring, I will say nothing."

"Well, Tate," I told him with a slight sigh. "I don't actually need you to say anything. Raulf here is going to get all of the information we need."

Tate stared at Raulf for several seconds. "I don't see how."

"Ah, well, you see, Raulf here is a Changeling."

Tate gave me a blank stare.

"Apart from weres like my friend Thomas over there…"

Thomas smiled and Tate flinched. Werewolves have that effect sometimes.

"As I was saying," I continued, "apart from weres there are several species in the world who can change their appearance. The three most common of these are Shaman, who can turn into several different types of animals, shape shifters, who can change their own physiology as they see fit, and changelings who can become other people."

The import of this information dawned on Tate very quickly. "You're going to replace me with him."

I nodded.

"No one will believe he's me!"

"Actually they will," I corrected. "Because, you see, when changelings become someone else, they absorb their memories and traits along with their physical appearance. Raulf will, for all intents and purposes, *be* you in every single way that matters. He'll still retain his own personality and independent thought, but your memories and life will be right there with him. He'll actually be a better you. He won't cheat on his wife or murder staff members because he was too stupid not to get caught in a treasonous plot. By the way, it was good of you to send your wife and child away, we'd have had a much harder time arranging this if they were here."

"But what happens to me?" Tate eventually managed to stammer.

"When a changeling absorbs someone else, they absorb their features too. You'll be turned into a smooth, pink, fleshy bag with descriptive marks. Your body will be disposed of by whatever carrion-eaters we happen to have working in the city." I walked toward the door. "Thomas and I will be outside," I said to Raulf. "Are you sure you're up to this?"

"It is my honor to serve Avalon in this way," he said with a slight nod of the head. "The process will take some time."

"Good-bye, Lord Tate," I said. "If you hadn't been such a colossal waste of a title, you may never have met us. As it is, this is your own fault."

"Mordred," Tate shouted, gaining my utmost attention.

"What did you just say?" I demanded.

"When Buckingham met me to arrange everything, he mentioned working for another man. He called him Mordred, after the character from the King Arthur legend."

I darted toward Tate, grasped him around the neck, lifted him off the chair, and slammed him into the wall, his feet dangling uselessly above the wooden floor.

"Are you certain?" I asked. "Do not lie to me."

Tate nodded as best he could. "I can't tell you more though."

I released Tate and let him drop to the floor. "You'd be surprised what the mind can recall, even when you can't remember." I turned to Raulf. "Dredge his mind clean, search for anything about Mordred."

Raulf nodded and stepped toward the traitor as I walked out of the house with Thomas beside me, the screams of horror only reaching us as we closed the front door.

CHAPTER 4

The whole process took only an hour, but it was enough time for Thomas to run off and arrange for the Tate household to be cleaned and the bodies of the maid, butler and Tate himself to be disposed of.

While the Shield of Avalon had assigned Thomas to live in London and watch the tower, there were other agents within the city who were doing a similar job. All of them had an understanding, if you needed something removed or cleaned quickly; you could contact them. Occasionally the work of the SOA gets dark and dangerous, especially if they discover something, or someone, that needs stopping, or are in turn discovered. Being able to count on your comrades-in-arms to reduce exposure to yourself and your goals is a necessity. I didn't ask what species would be helping Thomas clean the house, or what they would do with the bodies and blood. There were some things better off unknown, but I was sure the three corpses would go toward feeding a few people for several weeks or months.

Left alone while Thomas made his arrangements, I paced up and down outside the house, impatient to learn more about Mordred's involvement. At one time I'd considered him a friend, although those days had long since passed. Centuries ago, Mordred, along with a woman I'd once loved, used me to get Arthur where they wanted and then attacked us both, nearly killing me and mortally wounding Arthur. Only Merlin's magic kept Arthur from immediate death. Since that day more and more magic is needed to keep Arthur in his state of neither living nor dead, as Merlin refuses to allow my friend and king to die without a fight.

Mordred disappeared immediately after the attack, occasionally turning up over the years to cause mayhem wherever he went and then vanishing for centuries after. The need for retribution to be visited upon Mordred had been coming for some time.

Hopefully, in stopping Mordred I would also learn the location of Ivy, a psychic whom Mordred had infected with dark blood magic, giving her an immortal lifespan, but one infused with constant torture and misery. I'd had the chance nearly seventy years previously to save her and stop Mordred, and I'd failed to do either. I swore that if I got the chance, I wouldn't fail again.

"Nathaniel, I want to know, too," Thomas said once he'd returned. "Mordred knows were Ivy is. I haven't forgotten her." Clearly he'd been having the same thoughts I'd had. Thomas had been seriously injured by Mordred's followers, allowing my old nemesis to escape into the French countryside with Ivy.

"But?" I asked.

"But your constant pacing and glaring at the house is making me nervous."

I took a deep breath and tried to calm my thoughts. Thomas was right, I needed to relax.

Unfortunately, Raulf, the new Lord Tate, had fallen asleep after the transfer was complete, and the hour turned into two before he resurfaced. The time had done very little to ease the anxious feeling that had settled inside me.

Raulf opened the front door and beckoned Thomas and me to join him in the study.

"How are you feeling?" Thomas asked as we entered the

room.

"Lord Tate was not a healthy man, but I've expunged all disease from my body and am ready to work as needed."

It was always weird to see a changeling after finishing the transformation, the fact that I'd been talking to the original lord only a few hours ago was a little disconcerting. "Are you ready to tell us what we need? What did you discover about Mordred?"

"Tate was telling the truth, Buckingham mentioned Mordred only once in his hearing. But there was something else in the memory, a tone of fear in Buckingham's voice. I believe that Mordred is definitely involved in the princes' disappearance. How much involved, I can't say."

"Anything else?" Thomas asked.

Raulf nodded. "Tate was told to meet some soldiers at a tavern near Gatton Park, south of here. He was to pass over the crowns and then ride on with them. He knew nothing more than that, not even their destination."

"A ditch, I imagine," I said.

"That's what I feel too," Raulf said. "Although Tate firmly believed he could trust them."

"What's the name of the inn?" Thomas asked.

"The Huntress," Raulf replied. "Tate was told that it was a fine establishment."

"I guess we ride south then," I said. "When was Tate meant to arrive?"

"Tomorrow evening, but your arrival sped up his planned departure. If you left now, you'd be there by nightfall."

I shook Raulf's hand. It was an odd sensation. "You are to act as Tate would have, but any information you gather is to be given to one of the SOA agents whom Thomas will inform you about."

"Yes, sir," Raulf said.

"And be nice to your wife, she didn't deserve to have a traitor as a husband, I imagine."

"I believe she knew nothing. And despite the fact that she is quite the striking woman, his list of sexual encounters with maids and whores is long and mostly unpleasant to think about."

"Well, this is a chance for Lord Tate to be the best husband in London."

I left Thomas and the new Lord Tate together to discuss whatever details needed to be arranged out and went to my horse. I'd taken the bag with the two crowns with me. Part of me had wanted to melt them down right away, but if the soldiers in the inn were expecting to receive crowns, I might be able to use them to find out where the princes were being taken.

Then there was the problem of Mordred. If he was involved and that possibility appeared to be very high, then it changed things. I knew that Mordred would only be part of anything if it meant the possibility of hurting Merlin, and by extension Avalon, but for the moment I doubted he had any notion of my investigation. I needed to keep it that way if I hoped to stop Mordred and his plans once and for all.

I attached the bag to my saddle and pulled myself up onto the animal, ready to calm the horse if necessary, once Thomas reappeared. As it turned out I needn't have been worried; Thomas arrived and the horse gave no indication that it was unhappy about it.

"You really have been practicing," I said.

"So long as I don't change, I can control it."

"And how are you going to keep up with me once we leave the city?"

"I don't think you need to worry about me being too slow." He paused for a second and a serious expression crossed his face.

"That bastard Mordred is involved. I want to kill him, Nathaniel. For what he and his friends did back in France, I want him to die painfully."

"We will find him," I said. "And he *will* tell us where Ivy is. Even if I have to remove one tiny piece of him at a time until he talks."

CHAPTER 5

Once we left the city, Thomas vanished into the woodlands that stretched for miles on either side of the road. Occasionally I had glimpses of Thomas darting through the trees, or a deer would sprint out in front of me, startled by the presence of a predator. I wished I could have joined him, using my air magic to make me faster and more agile, but keeping the horse was more important than exorcising the emotions I was feeling after discovering that Mordred was involved in the princes' disappearance. So, instead I spurred the horse on to a canter. I would have liked to go full gallop, but the ground was uneven, and I didn't want to risk the animal's health for the sake of arriving at the tavern sooner.

As it turned out, even with resting the horse twice, it still only took three hours to reach our destination.

A few hundred meters from the tavern, I got down from my horse and led him by the reins toward a nearby stable, hitching him to a post outside. After checking I was alone, I removed the satchel containing the crowns and walked into the stables, which was devoid of man or beast. I walked to the far end of the building and hid it under a large bale of hay. It wasn't the safest place on earth to hide something, but it would keep until I was ready to retrieve it.

I exited the stable with a hand full of hay and fed it to my horse, as a shirtless Thomas emerged from the woods. He was pulling his shirt out of a satchel and putting it on when I noticed he wasn't wearing shoes either. Werewolves don't like shoes at the best of times, and running in them was unheard of.

"You managed not to stop off for a meal," I said.

Thomas finished buttoning his shirt and removed his shoes from the bag, dropping them onto the damp ground. "I didn't think we had time," he said with a grin. "Although if you're saying we do, I could really go for some deer. I noticed plenty running away from me as I ran."

Drops of water fell onto my forehead. "I think getting out the coming rain is more important than your stomach."

The sound of raucous behavior reached me well before we'd covered the distance to the large tavern. It sat on two-floors, with the huge stable next to it.

If I'd thought the noise was loud outside, it was nothing compared to the cacophony of sound that exited through the open front door. At least a dozen soldiers, all wearing chainmail or leather armor, were busy drinking and laughing. The smell of cooked meat made my stomach growl, reminding me that I hadn't eaten for a while, and Thomas licked his lips and took a deep breath.

"You need food," I told him, which gained only a nod as we walked through the throng of armed men to the counter at the end of the room. A short, thin man with a large jaw and crooked nose stood behind the counter in conversation with a tall, elegant-looking woman. They stopped talking the second Thomas and I reached them, and both turned with a smile to greet us.

"Gentlemen, how can my wife and I be of assistance?" the man asked.

"Food," Thomas said with an almost growl.

"What are the soldiers eating?" I asked.

"Pork in a broth with vegetables. Everything we cook is

fresh. Would you gentlemen like the same?"

I nodded. "Can you bring it to our table along with some beer? Also, my horse is outside, can you ensure he's placed in the stables and properly cared for?"

The man nodded and scurried off through a door behind him, presumably to the kitchen. The wife smiled at me as a young, voluptuous woman arrived and motioned for me and Thomas to follow her. She led us away from the soldiers, a few of whom I noticed were now watching us.

"Are the innkeepers your parents?" I asked and removed my black cloak before taking a seat at the table.

She nodded. "Yes, they own the tavern."

"It's unusual to be taken to a seat," I said. "Normally one fends for one's self."

"The soldiers are very loud," she said softly. "I doubt you'd like your meal interrupted. Will you be staying the night?"

I shrugged. "That depends on the weather outside." I glanced out the nearest window as the rain began to increase.

She smiled and nodded, quickly walking away to deal with several of the soldiers who were beckoning her over.

"That is one very attractive, young woman," Thomas said. "Maybe this inn won't be so bad."

One of the soldiers had pulled the young woman onto his lap and was busy trying to get a kiss, an act that got him a slap from the woman and riotous laughter from his friends as she walked away.

I stopped watching at that moment when another servant, clearly the sister of the one who'd shown us to our seats, brought over two huge bowls of succulent pork, placing them in front of Thomas and me.

"Enjoy," she said as her mother placed two mugs of beer on

the table.

"I will, thank you," I said. Thomas would have said something, but he'd already started tearing into the thick strips of pork and drinking the broth that they sat in. "Can you bring over two more bowls?" I asked.

The wife nodded and walked away with her daughter in tow. Something was very odd about that family. I wondered what it may have been and settled on the fact that maybe they were foreign. It was certainly possible. Apart from the father, their accents weren't quite English, but they appeared to speak the language without difficulty. It was entirely possible that they assumed people would be less comfortable being served by a foreign family.

I'd just finished my first bowl of hot pork and broth, when the wife brought over the second. "That was excellent," I said.

"Thank you," she said with a slight bow of her head. "It's something I learned to cook a long time ago."

"Did you learn it in Asia?"

The wife looked taken aback for a few seconds, and even Thomas stopped drinking the broth from his rapidly diminishing second bowl to look over at me.

"You've been to Asia?" she asked, slight anxiety in her voice.

"I spent a lot of time in China; I've been to Japan too. Lovely countries, although the Japanese tend to distrust strangers."

"I wasn't aware any foreigners had officially been to Japan," she said, cautiously.

"Ah, well *officially*, Japan hasn't been visited by the west. But we've been, just not *en masse*. They're skeptical of outsiders and sometimes that turns into distrust or anger. But you're not Asian in appearance, so you must have travelled there yourself."

"I spent time in China as a child. My parents were merchants, so travel was necessary. I leaned a good many recipes from all over."

"Judging by the crowd of soldiers, your cooking must be in great demand."

The wife smiled. "We are not normally this busy."

"Any idea why they're here?" Thomas asked nonchalantly. "There's no danger, is there?"

"I don't think so. They mentioned they were waiting for an important man to show. I think they're just biding their time and letting off some steam."

"Well, in addition to the good food, this is excellent beer." Thomas held up his empty mug to prove his point.

"That's true, it's excellent," I agreed, finishing my own mug.

"Two more?" the wife asked.

We both nodded.

"What's wrong?" Thomas asked when we were alone.

"Something weird is happening here."

"Ah, Nathaniel, relax. We're being served excellent food and drink by beautiful women. I think that's a pretty good way to spend an evening. Tomorrow we'll hunt down Mordred and Buckingham, rescue the boys, and then find Ivy."

"You're very sure of yourself."

"If I doubt it, I'll just start to worry and over-think things. I need to be able to control myself when I see Mordred. Tearing him in half before he tells us what we need won't help anyone except me."

I sighed and nodded slightly. "You're right. I'm probably just tired and anxious about the fact that we need to find those princes before Buckingham and Mordred can finish their plan."

"Well we can't go anywhere until we figure out where those crowns were meant to be taken."

It was a good point.

"You do know that the second we go speak to those soldiers, it's not going to end politely." A sly grin spread across Thomas lips.

"You'd best finish enjoying your food and drink first. I'm hoping that if they keep drinking, any problems they can muster are going to be finished before they get serious."

CHAPTER 6

We spent several hours in the tavern, while the soldiers got louder and louder, and the rain outside turned into a downpour. Although I was in a hurry, I wanted to make sure that the soldiers were not only full of food and drunk on beer, but that there wouldn't be anyone else arriving.

What concerned me were the four men at the table farthest from the festivities. They were clearly soldiers and had watched Thomas and me from the second we'd entered the tavern. None of them had been drinking, and all four were avoided by the rest of the soldiers. I deduced that they were in charge and probably not people to underestimate.

"Are you ready?" I asked Thomas, who nodded.

We stood in unison, and I put my cloak back on before we made our way past the now-singing men to the table in the corner. As soon as we reached it the joviality behind us ceased. We were now the center of everyone's attention, no matter their inebriated status.

"Can we help you gentlemen?" a dark-haired man on the far side of the table asked, his voice low and gravelly.

"Tate sent us," I said, gaining no response from the men.

The man closest to Thomas shrugged, his long blond hair

falling over wide shoulders. "Don't know whom you mean."

"Look, I don't have time for this," I snapped. "Tate got nabbed by the king's guard, but managed to get a message to me to bring the items here. He didn't exactly have time to let me know the names of everyone I was to meet, just the destination."

"Is he dead?" the blond asked.

"I don't fucking know or care about his current status, I just want these damn things out of my sight. They're far too dangerous to be carting all over the land."

"Where are they?" the dark-haired man asked.

"Attached to the horse outside, I didn't want to risk bringing them in here. I didn't know whom I would be meeting. Glad to find you're all *such* upstanding soldiers."

All four men laughed, followed quickly by the rest of the soldiers. "Not been called upstanding in some time," the dark-haired man said. "Name's James, we're mercenaries."

"Well, at least you're not bandits," Thomas said.

"Hugh, go with our friend here to get the merchandise," James said to the blond mercenary, ignoring Thomas's comment.

"Come on," Hugh said, standing up and wrapping a cloak around his leather armor clad shoulders. "I don't want to be out in that rain all night."

"Your friend can take a seat and enjoy himself," James said, while the other two mercenaries at the table made a show of playing with the daggers they held. "It's not a request."

Thomas sat in Hugh's chair as requested, with a big grin on his face. A bunch of human mercenaries weren't going to be much trouble for either of us, but I preferred that it not come to that until the time was right.

I pulled the hood of my own cloak up and stepped out into the rainy night with Hugh beside me. We hurried to the stables, and I was grateful for the shelter they provided. Hugh waited for me by the building's entrance, while I walked to the still empty stall at the end of the stables, next to where my horse had been placed, and retrieved the satchel from under the bale of hay.

He held out his hand, and I passed the satchel over, whereupon he eagerly opened it to check the contents. "Is that it?" he asked.

I nodded. "What did you expect?"

"Something a bit more extravagant. It's for a king and a prince."

"Well apparently, extravagant is to be replaced with plain and functional. The king of the people."

Hugh closed the satchel and slung the strap over his shoulder. "Sounds stupid to me. Kings are meant to be divine; they're supposed to be our betters."

"You should tell that to James and his friends. I think they believe God made a mistake this time."

Hugh laughed. "James doesn't give two shits about the fucking king or his friends. He cares about getting paid. About all of us getting paid."

"So," I said with a slight sigh as we reached the stable doors. "Are you meant to kill me on the way back in or out here with the horses?"

"Figured that out, did ya? Smart man." He pulled a dagger from his belt. "This ain't nothin' personal, you understand."

"Yeah, it is," I told him and blasted him in the chest with gale of air that took him off his feet and threw him across the stables. He slammed against a thick wooden beam with a loud crack and fell to the ground limp and lifeless.

I walked over to him and checked, but as I'd guessed, he was already dead. His neck, and probably his back, was broken. I retrieved his dagger and the satchel before running back through the rain to the tavern.

"Where's Hugh?" James asked as I stepped through the front door. He was clearly surprised to see me.

I tossed the dagger onto the nearest table. "You're a nasty piece of shit getting Hugh to kill me once I'd handed over the crowns."

"You did what?" Thomas demanded of James in mock surprise. "Untrustworthy mercenaries, whatever next?"

"We have your friend," James reminded me.

"Yeah, that you do, you poor unlucky bastards. Make it quick, Thomas."

Thomas struck with a speed that no human could have matched, slamming his hand into the throat of the nearest mercenary and catching another in the jaw with an elbow that sent the man to the ground as the first man began to choke.

He caught James in the chest with a vicious kick, sending him sprawling to the floor. And then he slowly stood up and cracked his knuckles. Thomas was going to enjoy himself.

He head butted the first man who came too close, but held onto his shirt and threw him over a table onto the laps of several more of the mercenaries whose alcohol-addled minds had made them slow and uncoordinated to respond to the threat.

One of the men decided that I was an easier target and drew a knife, which soon clattered to the ground as I broke his arm and drove him face-first through the nearest table. I dropped the unconscious and bloody mercenary and stood back watching as even the drunkest of soldiers had decided that they needed to get involved, advancing on Thomas with swords drawn.

Within moments there were bodies and blades being thrown around the room. Thomas remained in human form, which kept the ensuing carnage from reaching the point where severed body parts started flying, but even so, I made sure to stay well out of the way.

The fight didn't last long; Thomas was far too strong and fast for anyone to land even a glancing blow. Besides, once you've been hit by a werewolf, you tend to stay where you fall. So, a few minutes later and Thomas was sitting on a table, holding one of the few remaining conscious mercenaries by his throat, before throwing him over a nearby pile of unconscious bodies.

"That was fun," Thomas said with a smile, climbing down and walking over to the table where we'd shared our dinner, to drink whatever remained of his beer.

I turned toward him, my back facing the door of the tavern. "Did you leave anyone in a condition to talk?" I asked.

"At least one," he said and pointed behind me.

I turned and found James standing by the door, holding one of the tavern owner's daughters by her arm in an iron grip.

He saw me and placed his sword against her throat. "We're leaving here," he announced.

"Or what?" I asked. "If you kill her, you'll die pretty soon afterwards."

"Yeah, but do you really want innocent blood on your hands?"

I thought for a second. I doubted I could get to him before he killed the woman. "I'm going to count to a hundred and then I'm coming after you. If I were you, I'd be as far from here as possible by then."

James opened the tavern door allowing the wind to whip inside, before dragging the terrified daughter out into the elements with him.

"What are you doing?" the mother screamed at me as the tavern's door slammed shut.

I turned to look at her. She was holding her second daughter in a tight embrace, anguish on her face.

"Please find my daughter," the father said, his voice shaking.

"Thomas stay here and make sure none of these men bother this nice family," I said. "If any of them are capable of speech, maybe find out where they were meant to go next."

"You sure you don't want me to track him?" he asked.

I shook my head. "He won't be hard to find, besides I have a few questions for him."

I wrapped my cloak around me and opened the tavern door.

"Please find my daughter," the mum wailed, mirroring her husband's words.

I didn't answer, instead stepping out into the night.

"Good hunting, Nathaniel," Thomas called behind me as the tavern door closed.

CHAPTER 7

Too much time had passed without finding James or his hostage, and I couldn't shake the feeling I'd missed something important. There were no horses in the stable, apart from my own, and he didn't have time to try and saddle it to ride off. Instead he'd taken to the woods.

Fortunately the rain had stopped, so for about fifty yards, his track had been easy to follow. He'd stuck to the well-walked path and I'd noticed the dragging marks from the woman he'd taken, but after that, his tracks had vanished. At first I had assumed he'd taken her further into the dense forest, but I was beginning to doubt that theory. There were no obvious breaks in the forest, and no disturbed plants or wildlife that I could find.

It should have been an easy search, should have been over and done with before James knew what had hit him. Instead, I was standing in the middle of a dark forest, my magic the only thing allowing me to see where I was going.

I decided the best course of action was to re-trace my steps and try to track James over again from there. It didn't take long to make my way back to where the tracks stopped, but once there I had the same problem. It was as if both James and the woman had vanished. Concern bubbled away inside me. Something was very wrong with this situation, but I couldn't quite figure out what. Maybe a predator had come this way. There were plenty of vampires or were-creatures in the south of England, and even the occasional giant or troll. I was suddenly very aware of how exposed I was and looked all around, only satisfied when I'd eliminated the possibility of an imminent attack.

I walked to a nearby massive elm tree and placed a hand against the trunk, which was sticky with something that held me fast. I pulled as hard as I could, but my hand remained stuck to the tree trunk. I ignited a fire in my palm that burned away whatever had trapped me, then held the fire close to the trunk, moving it over the bark until I caught a glimpse of whatever had held me fast. A web. The kind of spider-web that can hold a full-grown man captive.

An itch started at the base of my neck, and I knew that something was watching me from the tree-tops high above. I sensed movement directly above me and I slipped a hand to the silver dagger from my belt, palming it as I slowly took a step away from the base of the tree.

In one motion, I leapt back and threw the dagger up into the tree canopy. It connected with something solid and almost immediately there was a crashing sound as something heavy fell from high above me, hitting the ground moments later.

If James hadn't been dead before he'd been hoisted up into the leaves and branches, he was when he hit the ground head first after a fifty-foot-drop. His body was wrapped in the same kind of web that I'd burned away, but I dared not get any closer.

"He was my prey," a female voice said, although I couldn't pinpoint the exact direction it was coming from. "The stupid man shouldn't have taken me. They were meant to die in the tavern."

"The daughter of the tavern owners, I presume," I said to the darkness. "So, what are you? Because not a single member of your family is human."

"Very good," she said, and I heard scurrying across the branches from where James had fallen. "We are *jorōgumo*."

"Your mother really was Japanese then. You all are."

"We can change our faces enough to look English. And we have no problems making ourselves look beautiful as needed."

There was a crack above me, and, as I jumped back several feet, something made a thud on the ground almost exactly where I'd been standing. Even in the darkness I could see the monstrosity before me.

Jorōgumo are half spider, half human, although they're born looking like the latter and only start to evolve into the monster they become once they've taken their first victim. The more they devour, the faster and more complete the transformation. They can shift between a fully human appearance and their spider-human hybrid at will, although only doing so when hunting. Unfortunately, the only way of telling if the beautiful woman in front of you is a *Jorōgumo* is when she shifts her appearance, and by then it's far too late.

"Do I not look beautiful?" she demanded as she crept onto the path and stepped into better view. Her legs still numbered two, although they were now bare and dark in color. She also had two arms and two eyes, but out of each side of her jaw a mandible protruded, each with a razor sharp tip. They'd torn through the skin on her face as they'd exposed themselves.

"You're not fully grown," I said.

"No, I have a few feeds to go before that can happen. And as you ruined my fun with James, you get to take his place."

"I met some of your kind before," I said as I took a few tentative steps backward, putting distance between me and the speed and ferocity that I knew existed inside all *jorōgumo*. "They liked to kill people from a nearby village, or travelers who wandered too far into the woods. They don't do that anymore. They're now corpses on a hill." While my words were true, I left out that it hadn't been a good kill. I'd been seriously injured by one of the *jorōgumo* and had been forced to wait for several days while their extremely potent venom, a substance that seemingly bypassed my body's ability to heal and rendered my magic ineffective, worked its way out of my system.

I really began to wish I'd taken my *guan doa* with me when I'd left to travel to London. The six foot long halberd like weapon, with curved blade, would have been a much better weapon against a *jorōgumo* than my dagger would be.

"You won't find me easy to defeat," she said and clicked her mandibles together, the sound sending a shiver up my spine.

She took two steps and then launched herself in my direction. I managed to throw myself to the side, rolling over several plants as I retrieved and threw another of my silver daggers. The blade buried itself in the back of her shoulder and she screamed.

The *jorōgumo* turned on me and reached over her shoulder to remove the dagger, but couldn't quite manage it, so gave up in anger. "I'm going to enjoy this," she said and took another step forward, before pausing to stare as white glyphs lit up over my arms.

"I guess you noticed the glyphs," I said with a slight smile. The glyphs had shone through the ripped sleeves of my dark shirt the second I'd started sending out tendrils of air all along the ground toward the *jorōgumo*.

"I've never taken a sorcerer before. This will be fun."

"Not for you, it won't be." I snapped the tendrils up from the ground, hardening the air as it moved, the tendrils wrapping themselves around the legs and torso of the *jorōgumo*. Finding herself suddenly trapped, she thrashed and cursed me as the hardened air squeezed tighter and tighter, until she was finally forced to cease moving altogether.

"You can't keep me forever. And you can't possibly think that I will answer your questions. "

"I can keep you here long enough to get some answers from you."

"Release my daughter," said a voice from behind me.

I glanced over my shoulder to find the mother standing behind me.

"I don't really want to fight two *jorōgumo*," I said and turned back to the daughter, who had begun to smile and click her mandibles together.

The sound of tearing and an occasional groans of pain from the direction of the mother told me that she was changing from her human shape.

"You can release her and die quickly as a man, or you will become our next family meal, and your death will be slow and agonizing." The mother's voice was deeper than before and punctuated with the same clicking noise that the daughter had been doing with her mandibles.

I kept my prisoner in place as I turned back to the mother. She was no longer the beautiful woman from the tavern; she was a fully grown *jorōgumo*. From waist to neck, she still looked like a woman. She'd torn away her clothes and her naked skin glistened as the moonlight caught it. But her face was a ruined mess. Like her daughter, she had two large mandibles that had ripped through the skin along her jaw line, but she also had two fangs that protruded from the top of her mouth, which had all but destroyed her top lip. For a second I could have sworn that I'd seen something drip from one of them onto her bare chest. *Jorōgumo* venom was one of the most potent I'd ever encountered; nothing on earth would have tempted me to willingly be near those fangs ever again.

The mother's legs, now dark and covered in hair, hung a foot above the ground dangling from a huge, black, spider's abdomen with six more legs, all of which ended with a small claw. Part human, part spider and a truly formidable killing machine.

"There's a third option," I said and released the wind magic holding the younger *jorōgumo* in place. She fell to her feet with a smile of victory on her face that lasted only seconds until a blade of air that protruded from my closed fist caught her in the throat. I twisted the blade and stepped aside as I tore it free, almost decapitating her.

Blood exploded from the massive wound and a blast of air threw her into her mother, whose screams filled the forest more completely than her daughter's earlier attempt had managed.

The mother swatted the corpse aside with one of her huge legs, sending it into a nearby tree, as she charged at me. I stood my ground until the last second, then threw myself aside and rolled to my feet.

Orange glyphs flared to life on my arm as I ignited a whip of fire from each hand and brought one down on the *jorōgumo's* leg, severing the limb. The smell of burnt flesh permeated the area, as she cried out. The second whip lashed out at the monster, but she darted away from me and quickly scurried up a nearby tree.

My two whips of flame touched the ground, scorching the soft earth, but not starting a fire. I would have usually snuffed their flame and conserved my magic, but I had no idea how long I had before the *jorōgumo* re-emerged and attacked anew.

"This leg will take time to grow back," she cursed from her hidden vantage point.

I remained quiet and tried to pinpoint where she was.

"You murdered my daughter. My eldest child. You'll pay for that."

I wanted to use my air magic to search her out, but that would have required pulling back my fire, which would, in turn, have put me at a considerable disadvantage, and I couldn't risk it. One bite from her fangs and I was as good as dead.

"I'm going to suck your marrow," she taunted, probably trying to get some sort of reaction from me.

"So are you angrier that you lost a leg or that you allowed

your daughter to die? Great parenting skills you have there," I said, hoping to make her obvious anger boil over into action.

"You want to see parenting? Allow me to show you."

There was a scurrying sound from above me that suddenly stopped as the tree tops began to rustle and sway.

"It's time to get your fill," the *jorōgumo* said.

For a brief second I wondered what she was talking about. It wasn't until I saw the first spider began to lower itself from the branches above that I realized her last few words hasn't been directed to me at all. I removed the whips of fire; they weren't going to be any real help now.

The *jorōgumo* dropped below the dense leaves and began to make her way down the tree trunk. "I may only have a few human-looking children, but I've also given birth to thousands of my beautiful little darlings. They're only babies, but I wonder if any of them have the power to kill you. I guess we'll see."

One of the spiders, roughly the size of my hand, was a little too enthusiastic and leapt toward me. A quick swipe up with a hastily formed blade of fire severed it in two, each half making a sickening noise as it struck the ground.

"You can't kill them all," The *jorōgumo* said, sounding far too cheerful about my situation.

I sprinted across to a large tree that appeared to be devoid of the little bastards, narrowly dodging several more large spiders that decided I was going to be their next meal. I needed some space, somewhere I could stand and prepare for the onslaught. When I reached the tree, there was twenty feet between me and the spiders, as dozens of them continued their descent until the sound of them dropping onto the earth was all I could hear.

"Goodbye, sorcerer," the *jorōgumo* said. "I'll be sure that your friend dies much more quickly than you will."

I'd picked this tree for my final stand, simply because of the lack of plants directly in front of it or around it. About ten feet of bare earth surrounded the trunk. I glanced up, but saw no spiders moving toward me. I didn't feel very lucky about the ones crawling along the ground in my direction, but having them in front of me was a hell of a lot better than having them come from all sides.

As I waited for the inevitable attack, I removed another dagger from my belt and took a deep breath.

"You're going to fight all of my babies with that little thing?" the *jorōgumo* asked and began laughing.

I ignored her taunts and watched the ground directly before me, controlling my breathing until I was ready. The first spider appeared moments later, closely followed by the next dozen and the dozen after that. I breathed out, and then I drew the blade across my palm.

The cut was deep and blood poured freely from the wound. I brought both hands together, the dark blood magic glyphs joining those of my fire magic, and I unleashed an inferno. A wave of fire, hot enough to destroy everything in its path, swept out thirty feet in front of me, igniting everything it touched. Nothing withstood its onslaught, and when I was certain that all of the spiders before me were nothing but ash, I raised my hands and the wave shot up into the treetops, incinerating anything living or dead. It consumed any remaining spiders, along with the trees and leaves they lived within. The *jorōgumo's* screams were audible for a moment and then went silent.

I stopped the magic minutes later, completely extinguishing the fire. The nearby trees had turned to black husks, no longer capable of sustaining life. The very ground beneath my feet was a smoldering ruin, scarred beyond recognition. And yet, all of the trees and plant life beyond the thirty foot mark remained untouched.

In the center of the smoking circle of destruction was a cocoon of web, tainted black with the fire that had destroyed the *jorōgumo's* offspring. It was far too small to contain the monster in her transformed guise, but any fears I had were soon confirmed with when a red, blistered hand ripped through the web, freeing the human seeming *jorōgumo* inside.

She was burned down one side of her face, the skin bright red and raw, and blisters rippled along the exposed flesh of her neck and chest. Blood oozed from dozens of cuts, presumably from where she'd fallen through the trees before hitting the burning ground. She coughed up blood and dropped to one knee.

I readied myself to kill her, thinking she was mortally wounded and had little time left. But she saw me advance and sprang back into the still-living trees of the nearby forest, disappearing from view.

I should have gone after her, ended the problem once and for all. But Thomas was still at the tavern, and I was suddenly very concerned that he'd had an even worse time of it than me.

CHAPTER 8

I'd expected to find Thomas in the middle of a huge fight for his life, fending off at least the other daughter, who must also be a *jorōgumo*. Instead I entered the tavern and found him leaning up against the counter, a mug of ale in one hand and what appeared to be a chicken leg in the other.

Blood had been splattered all around the room, and many of the soldiers that Thomas had subdued earlier in the night appeared to have died in the time I'd been fighting in the woods.

"What happened?" I asked, eyeing the man tied to a chair with thick rope, a potato sack over his head, his clothing giving away that it was the tavern-owner.

"The soldiers woke up just as that lovely girl became a spider-monster."

"*Jorōgumo*," I said.

"That's the thing. Fortunately, she came down with a nasty case of decapitation before she could bite me. Several of the soldiers decided to attack me too. A few survivors ran away. I guess we could hunt them down."

"I don't think that'll be necessary," I said and noticed the bare feet of the waitress sticking out from behind the counter. I moved aside slightly and discovered her head was several feet away. "I was hoping to get some answers."

"Ah, well I left this one alive," Thomas said and pulled the sack off the head of the tavern-owner, where he was tied to the chair.

His face was similar to the female *jorōgumo* I'd faced earlier. The mandibles clicked against one another angrily. "Release me, at once," he said, his voice coarse and deep.

"You're not as strong as your wife, are you? She would have broken free by now. Which leaves the question of why don't you change back to human?"

His eyes darted to the door. "Is she alive? Please tell me you killed her. I'm not changing back if there's a chance she's still out there. I'm stronger like this."

"Male spiders are smaller than the female," I said. "I guess that carries over to your species. Although, don't some females eat the male after sex?"

"Really?" Thomas asked. "Wow, even I think that's disgusting. And I just tore someone's head off."

"We only mate when she's already feeding," the man said. "It's the only safe way to be sure she won't attack me."

"I bumped into the rest of your offspring in the forest," I told him. "There were a lot of them. If you produce so many children, why do you only have two grown daughters?"

"Only the most powerful will grow enough to become able to change shape." He glanced at the door again. "Are all of them dead?"

I nodded.

Instead of looking angry, or even upset, he appeared relieved and after a second, changed back into his human form, the skin on his face healing over instantly. "My days were numbered the second those babies were born. In the past, I'd managed to avoid the younglings until they'd matured enough not to consider me a threat, but I couldn't do it forever."

"Your own kids will eat you?" Thomas asked.

"When I'm too old to remain more powerful than them, yes they will. If there's one thing animals and *jorōgumo* both do, it's prey on the weak. It's one of the reasons I got my family to move away from Japan, fewer *jorōgumo* means a greater chance of living another year."

"Okay, enough of this," I snapped. "What was the plan supposed to be?"

"I have no idea what you're talking about."

I reached to my belt for a small dagger, but found none there. I'd need to replenish my supply at some point. Thomas must have sensed my intention, as he growled, long, low and threatening.

The small man reacted as if he'd actually been stabbed, almost launching himself back. I decided I was done playing nice and caught the chair with my foot, flipping it over onto its back. With an audible crack, the man's head connected with the wooden floor.

"Shall we try again?" I asked.

"Tate was supposed to bring the crowns here," the man said. "These soldiers were working for Buckingham. They were going to kill Tate and take the crown to Eastbourne, southeast of here, where they'd meet up with the rest of Buckingham's forces and rendezvous with a ship off the coast. The boys and the crowns are to sail for France."

"How do you know that?" Thomas asked.

"Drunken soldiers like to talk."

"And what was your role in all of this?" I asked.

"Someone hired us to make sure the soldiers and crowns

never left here. We're not part of whatever plan Buckingham has for those crowns, or the boys. The crowns were our payment for ensuring the soldiers died."

"Who hired you?"

"I've no idea what his name is."

Thomas growled again, and the man flinched. "He said his name was Mordred. He was about your height," he tipped his chin toward me. "But not as broad. Long dark hair. That's all I saw. He was the one who told Buckingham to send Tate here to meet the soldiers."

"If Mordred and Buckingham are working together, why does he want these soldiers? They're meant to deliver the crowns, why doesn't Mordred want them arriving?" I asked.

"You'd have to ask him that," the man said. "Our involvement ended with what we were paid to do."

"My guess is you'd do it whether you were paid or not," Thomas said. "How many people have come through those doors and never left?"

"I don't know," he said. "Fifty, sixty?"

"In how many years?" I asked.

"Four," he told us. "Look, I know you think we're monsters, but it's only natural for us to prey on the unsuspecting and the weak. It's what *jorōgumo* do."

"And what I do is kill people who do just that," I told him, and he flinched away from me. "But today is your lucky day. You've been honest, and quite frankly, I don't want to sully myself with killing you."

"Thank you," he said with an awful smile.

"Oh, you probably don't want to be smiling." I picked up the satchel, which had fallen on the floor at some point during the night's commotion and checked that the crowns were still secure.

"We're not untying you."

"You're just going to leave me here?" he asked incredulously.

"That's the plan. I don't want you running off and alerting anyone, so here you stay." I created a small ball of fire in one hand and threw it on the nearest soldier's body, which immediately caught fire. Several more balls of fire followed and soon there were the beginnings of an inferno on one side of the tavern. "But no one will ever be taken by you or yours here again. You probably have an hour until this building burns down. From the look of your wife when I left her in the woods, fire doesn't agree with your species."

"She's alive?" he asked, fear in his eyes as he struggled against the ropes.

I nodded. "Good luck."

Thomas and I stepped outside, leaving the smell of burning flesh and wood behind us, and I got my horse from the stable. When I returned a few minutes later, Thomas was watching the woods with concern.

"There's something out there. Something that smells of burnt flesh and death."

"The female *jorōgumo*," I said and swung up onto the horse. "He's in the house," I shouted into the woods. "He stood by while your other daughter died. You probably don't have long until the fire burns the house down, but if you're looking for revenge on him, you have time."

A series of clicks was the only reply I heard.

"A word of warning, "I added for her benefit. "If it's me you're after. I will take your head and move on with my day. My patience has been tested one time too many, and I do not have time to play any more games."

I nudged the horse forward.

"What if she sets him free and they run away together?"

Thomas asked after we'd made it a few hundred meters up the road.

I stopped the horse and turned back in time to see a dark shape sprint across the clearing from the woods to the tavern. A few seconds later, screams sounded in the breaking dawn.

"I guess I wasn't her top priority. Either way, she didn't have long to live with the injuries she'd sustained."

"Pretty awful way to die," Thomas said and the sound of the collapsing building signaled the end of the tavern.

"No more awful than being eaten alive by one of them. Quite frankly, I'd say it was the death they deserved."

CHAPTER 8

"Why aren't we heading for Eastbourne?" Thomas asked after it became increasingly apparent that we were going in the wrong direction.

"We need to see someone first," I told him, as he walked beside the horse. "So, we'll have to stop off in Brighton."

"Whom are we meeting?"

"An old… acquaintance. If those boys are being taken to France, there's no way that a ship of the size necessary to travel there is going to be anchored and just waiting. Safer for the ship to be further out to sea and just use a row boat to come ashore."

"So, once we find the ship, your acquaintance will get us onboard?"

"Not exactly, he's going to be there primarily to make sure the ship doesn't set sail before the princes are safe. He'll hopefully give Mordred and anyone working with him, something much more worrying than either of us. That should give us time to ambush them."

"And how will he do all of that?"

I wasn't exactly sure how much to tell Thomas, but anyone who had fought beside and for me the way he had deserved to know what we were about to get into. "He's a summoner," I told him.

Thomas stopped walking and stared up at me. "I didn't think there were any left."

"Most of them don't advertise anymore. That much power scares people, and scared people tend to do stupid things. Most summoners have either moved on to more remote places or hide their talents. The man who lives at Brighton is one of the few who does neither of those things."

"What type of summoner is he?"

"Water," I told him. Summoners came in a four different guises; fire, air, earth and water.

"I've never met one before. Anything I need to know?"

I thought about it for a second before answering. "Firstly, despite their lengthy lifespan of several centuries, they can be killed by anything a human can. It's why most of them are very cautious about showing their power. So, be aware that he might need protecting until he starts his work, but once he merges with the element he can't be hurt.

"Secondly, once he starts to work, get as far away from him as possible. Whatever he summons won't always be able to distinguish between friend and foe. Although he's more powerful than most, that only means he can summon something for a longer period of time. How much control he has comes down to his mental stamina."

"That it? Keep him safe and then get out of the way?"

"Oh, one last thing. Don't judge his entire species on his tendency to be a money-grabbing little bastard."

Before Thomas could ask more, we reached the outskirts of the small fishing village of Brighton. I'd heard of plans to expand the area into the beginnings of a town, but wasn't sure the few hundred people who lived and worked in the seas off the coast would be too happy with the resulting influx of people, many of whom would be rivals to their livelihood.

We continued to make our way through the village, garnering the occasional glance from one of the villagers, who were either tending to their land or weaving nets for the next fishing trip.

I climbed down from my horse and led him further into the village and up to the large stone house in the center. A large man appeared, struggling with a sheepskin fleece that was draped over his shoulders. His big, bushy, orange beard was at odds with his bald head, and appeared to be compensating for the lack of warmth on the top of his skull.

"I'm the sheriff of this village and am in charge here," he bellowed, the voice matching the man. "What do you need?"

A man riding his own horse was something of a rarity. It signaled that you were either very wealthy or a thief. The fact that Thomas was walking beside me put me firmly in the first category in the sheriff's eyes, thieves don't usually have someone to walk alongside their horse.

"I'm here to see someone," I told him as tied my horse to a nearby post. "And my horse requires food and water. It's been a long few hours."

"I'm in no mood to…" the sheriff began, quickly quieting down when I tossed him a small pouch of gold coins. "My Lord," he said with a slight bow. "Your horse will be attended to. May I ask whom you're here to visit; maybe we can be of service."

"We're here to see Alan."

The sheriff blanched at the mention of the summoner's name, and I noticed several of the villagers stop what they were doing to turn and stare at Thomas and me.

"He lives on a house by the sea front," one of the villagers said, a small woman with a pale complexion and bright red cheeks. "Are you here to take him from us?"

The slight note of pleading in her voice led me to believe that Alan wasn't the most popular person in Brighton.

"That depends on him. But maybe, yes."

"He's in the house right now," the sheriff said. "He doesn't leave unless it's important."

"How many people live here?" Thomas asked.

"Four hundred and nine," he said. "I make sure to count."

"How many does Alan take money from?" I asked.

"Anyone who wants to be able to go to sea and return home safely," the woman told us. "We pay him, or our ships are destroyed. He tells us that he keeps all the boats safe when they're out on the water. He's full of dark magic."

"So, you rely on him to keep you all safe. In fact, you pay him to do just that, but don't actually want to be anywhere near him?" Thomas asked.

"Like I said, dark magic," the woman said and made the sign of the cross over her chest.

I nodded thanks to the sheriff and villagers and, after removing the satchel from my horse, Thomas and I made our way through the village toward the sea. The summoner's house wasn't hard to spot. To start with, it was massive, a three-floor building made of huge pale stones. But more than its size was the simple fact that it was the only dwelling anywhere near the water.

We walked across the beach and stopped outside the house, where I started to knock on the thick wooden door. It took a few times before anyone decided to recognize the fact that we were outside.

"Fuck off," came a gruff voice from the floor above, followed by the unmistakable sound of a woman's moan.

"Alan, you can answer the door, or I can break it down," I shouted. "Whatever runes you have will do more damage to your home than to me."

I counted to sixty as another moan, this one high pitched and urgent, sounded out, followed by a deep bellow of pleasure.

"I could have lived a long, happy life and not heard that." Thomas said.

"If that's the worst thing he says or does today, count yourself lucky."

I stepped back from the door to the sound of bolts being thrown from inside the house. Eventually the door opened, to reveal a tall, muscular man with long, dark hair that flowed over his shoulders, where more dark hair continued. He was also sweaty and naked.

"You could have put something on," I said as he moved aside to let Thomas and me into his warm house.

The room we stepped into was steeped in finery. Statues and busts sat on ornate tables and a wolf rug lay on the cold stone floor.

"You've done well," Thomas said, lifting up a handful of gems from a nearby bowl.

"Are you here for a cut or something?" he asked.

"Alan, do you remember me?" I asked.

"Nathaniel Garrett. You still work for that asshole Merlin?"

I ignored the taunt. I wouldn't get into an argument with him. It was a worthless pursuit. "I need your help."

"The answer is no," he said. "I'm quite happy. Now if you'll both leave, the sheriff's wife isn't going to fuck herself." He stopped and thought for a second. "Actually she might, she's quite the handful."

"You have the sheriff's wife up there?" Thomas asked. "No wonder he doesn't like you."

"Yeah, well he should pleasure his woman more often, instead of drinking himself into a stupor. She's a young, virile woman, and she needs a damn fine cock in her at every opportunity."

He motioned to his penis in case we didn't understand that he meant himself. I was pretty certain that anyone on earth would have understood without the need for a mime.

"You're clearly quite the catch," I said. "But you need to come with us."

"Did you not hear me? Agnes, come down here," Alan called out. And on cue a voluptuous, young woman came down the stairs, just as naked as Alan.

"Isn't she a beauty?" Alan asked, and slapped Agnes, who was presumably the sheriff's wife, on the ass.

She giggled, and then he kissed her forcibly, grabbing hold of one of her large breasts and squeezing it.

"Alan, you can either stay here and try to fuck your woman in front of us, which I assure you is neither impressive nor advised, or you can come with us and make some money."

Alan whispered to Agnes, who nodded toward Thomas and me before running back upstairs with another giggle.

"Any chance you have a red-hot poker?" Thomas asked. "I wish to blind myself."

"Fucking funny man," Alan snapped. "Now you said something about money."

I removed the satchel from my shoulder and threw it over to him. He caught it one handed and looked inside. "Crowns? What is this shit?"

"It's meant to be the crowns for the new king and prince of England. They need to be removed from sight and disposed of. They're your payment for helping. I assume you know people who will do this and pay you a good price for the gold and such?"

"That's a big price. What's the job?"

I saw no reason to lie to him, but no reason to tell him everything either. "Buckingham took the princes from the tower. He plans to take them to France. The result will be civil war here. Again."

"I heard Richard murdered the princes to secure the throne."

"You heard wrong," Thomas told him.

"Buckingham is a fucking idiot," Alan said. "He couldn't find fire if he set his own balls aflame. There's no way he's behind this."

I decided not to inform Alan of Mordred's involvement. At least not until he was too far involved to back out. "And yet, he's involved in this. So, are those crowns enough to gain your services?"

Alan licked his lips. It was more disturbing than the sex show earlier had been. "I need to get dressed. Give me ten minutes, and I'll find you down by the water."

I nodded and ushered Thomas out of the house. The wind carried the sounds of loud sex all the way across the beach and down to the water's edge, once we'd reached it.

"Does he really have time for that?"

"He can either get it out of his system now, and we'll have a lot easier time of it, or he's going to be even more insufferable to deal with."

"He's not exactly what good ladies dream of marrying."

"No, he's not, that's true. But I didn't hire him for his ability to be a gentleman."

"What about his ability not to sell us out at first chance?"

"He's been paid and handsomely. He'll see it through to the end, even if it means making enemies in the process. He's weirdly honorable like that."

"Do you really think he's keeping the village safe?"

I nodded. "For a fee, he's ensuring every ship that goes out comes back. What the villagers probably don't know is that he's the one putting the monsters out there in the first place."

*****

The ten minute wait turned into thirty, after which a thankfully dressed Alan emerged from his den of sexual gratification.

"Sorry," Alan said without ever sounding like he knew what the word meant. "Sometimes you've just got to finish up, you know?"

Thomas and I ignored his comment, and together we walked back up toward the village, only to be met by an irate-looking sheriff.

"Where's my wife?" he demanded to know.

"Exhausted," Alan said with an exaggerated sigh. "Probably a little sore too."

The sheriff's face grew red with anger and he stepped toward the summoner, a dagger in his hand.

I interjected myself between the two men. "You don't want to do that," I told the sheriff.

"He fucks my wife and then he has the gall to rub my nose in it, why the hell shouldn't I gut him like a fish?"

"I thought he kept your ships safe?" I asked.

"That's not enough for me anymore. I may be old, but I'm not going to stand back and let him humiliate me like this!"

Part of me wanted to step aside and watch Alan get destroyed, he certainly deserved it. But there were bigger things at stake. "But you will, because I need him. So, put your knife away and we'll pretend this never happened. Or, keep your knife out, and I'll take it from you. I promise you, only one of those options will allow you to keep your hand afterwards."

The sheriff stared at me with crazy eyes. "You think I'm scared?"

"I think you've reached the limit of patience. I think you're drunk too. Maybe if you stopped the latter, the former wouldn't happen."

"I'm not drunk," he assured me as the smell of stale alcohol reached my nose.

"Yes, you are. You're also beginning to draw a crowd of people, who will kill you if they think you're jeopardizing their livelihood. They may not like or trust him, but they like making money and having food on their plates."

Some semblance of sense dawned on the sheriff and he quickly hid the dagger, allowing the three of us to pass into the village, where several people asked Alan if he'd be back. He assured them that he would, that their ships would be safe while he was gone, but that they should keep his payments aside until he returned. He asked one man, a farmer, if he could have his horse, and the man quickly agreed.

"I'm so loved," he said with absolute smugness as I retrieved my own horse and led him out of the village.

When we were out of sight from the villagers, I passed Thomas the reins to my horse and then grabbed Alan by the throat, slamming him up against the nearest tree. "I want to make something very clear to you, you absolute bastard. I don't care who you fuck or who you piss off, but if your behavior endangers our job, I will let anyone who wants to cut you into tiny pieces. Are we clear?"

Alan nodded and I released my grip, letting him drop to his knees, coughing and spluttering.

"One more thing," I told him as I climbed up onto my horse.

"If you have thoughts of betrayal, be assured I will remove your testicles and give them to the sheriff of that village as a keepsake."

Alan nodded, but continued to smile. "You're not much fun, are you?"

"Alan, I know a great many ways to enjoy myself. On the other hand, if you piss me off again, you will almost certainly not share my enthusiasm for the fun methods I choose to employ on you."

"So, what's the plan, boss?" Alan asked as he climbed onto his horse and the three of us set off.

"We're going to Eastbourne. When we arrive, I want you to find out where their ship is. Thomas and I will look around the village for signs of the princes. It's not a large place, probably a bit bigger than Brighton, so it shouldn't take long."

"And if the princes are on the ship?"

"We retrieve them," I said. "Without damage."

"And once they're safe?" Alan asked with a gleam of mischief in his eye.

"Then the ship and its contents are yours. No survivors."

Alan's grin grew wide. It was not pleasant, nor did it give me hope that he would behave professionally once the violence started.

CHAPTER 9

It wasn't a very long journey, which was fortunate, as the English weather had turned increasingly unpleasant the closer we got to the village of Eastbourne.

By the time we reached the outskirts of our destination the cold wind was whipping into us with ferocity, and the rain was falling as if we were standing under a waterfall. I thought about using my magic to shield myself from the worst of it, but that was a frivolous use of magic, and one I didn't need. Better to just get on with it. We climbed a sizeable nearby hill, using the elevated position to look down on the fishing village a few hundred meters away, as we remained hidden by dense forest.

"There are a lot of soldiers down there," Thomas said. "They're wearing civilian clothes, but they're definitely soldiers."

"Weapons?" Alan asked.

"Swords, halberds, and bows. No horses and nothing we should be too concerned about. I count twenty men." A werewolf's vision was substantially better than either Alan's or my own.

"What about the ship?" I asked.

"There are several boats docked, most look like fishing boats. There are three small rowing boats sitting on the beach. I can't see very far out to sea, though, the rain obscures my vision too much."

"How close to the sea do you need to be to work?" I asked Alan.

"The closer the better. Too far away and I won't have much control. And trust me when I tell you that you want me to be able to control it."

"Thomas, go with Alan. The second those soldiers see either of you, they're going to come running. I want as many of them away from the village as possible when I get there, just in case one of them tries to use the princes as a bargaining tool."

"No problem," Thomas said. "How badly can I hurt them?"

"Whatever you need to do. By the time you're finished any soldiers will be dead, so won't be around to tell any stories about what they saw."

"What about the villagers?" Thomas asked. "I don't see any-one out and about, but that doesn't mean they're not there."

"They're probably inside several of the houses, out of the way. Buckingham wouldn't want anyone to get away and inform the King's men. Either that or they've all been killed. But then wip-ing out several hundred people is going to draw attention at some point, and they're waiting for the crowns."

"So, what you're saying is, you don't know if the villagers are dead or alive," Thomas said.

"It doesn't matter. If they're alive then maybe a few of them can be saved once the soldiers are dealt with, and if they're dead it won't matter what happens," Alan said. "Either way the plan is the same."

He had a good point. "We'll deal with the villagers when we need to. Both of you get to work. You won't have long before those soldiers decide you don't belong there."

Thomas shook my hand and walked off. Alan got down from his horse and allowed it to wander into the woods.

I pointed to one of the row boats beside a small pier that stretched out a few dozen feet into the sea. "I'll clear out any remaining guards from the village and wait on the end of the pier. If those boys are on that ship, I want them delivered to me as soon as possible."

Alan nodded in agreement. "That shouldn't be a problem."

I watched as Thomas and Alan made their way down the hill toward the sea. It didn't take long for the soldiers to notice them. Someone shouted and soon after, a dozen or so raced to intercept them, just as Alan walked a few feet into the water and knelt down.

Thomas changed into his werewolf beast form and began killing the soldiers with impunity. Several more soon ran out of the village to join the fight, but no one got any closer to Alan while the mass of werewolf muscle and razor sharp claws and teeth stood in their way.

I allowed my own horse to wander freely into the woods, before running toward the village, making sure to keep out of the line of sight of any of the soldiers currently fighting for their lives. And losing.

As I entered the village, a lone soldier saw me, but never had time to draw his sword as a flick of my wrist sent a blade of fire into his throat. By the time I reached him, he was already dead, but I caught him from falling to the ground and making more noise, and then hid his body behind two huge, sealed barrels.

Two more guards stood around the side of a modest-sized house, their backs facing me. Both died before they had time to realize they were in any danger, and another died when he had the misfortune to open the door to the house opposite at the very moment I stepped away from the two bodies.

I wrapped air magic around all three bodies and dragged them into the two-room house, which already held a dead man and woman. Apparently, the slaughter of the village's inhabitants had already begun.

I watched through the window of the house as several more guards left buildings and started off in the direction of Alan and Thomas. For a moment I wondered how Alan was doing, and then I heard a roar from the direction of the ocean. It was deafening and, even without seeing it, I was certain belonged to a predator the likes of which no one in the village would have ever seen before.

A summoner's talent lies in using his element to control monsters. Where those monsters come from is a mystery summoners are not forthcoming about, but once they have merged with the element itself, they gain control over the summoned monster. How much control and how powerful the beast they can summon depends on their own limits of power, but even the lowliest summoner can control creatures that cause utter destruction. And Alan was more powerful than most.

In the distance, I saw something rise out of the ocean and crash back down, causing a massive wave. Another roar sounded and I knew Alan was trying to control the beast he'd summoned forth.

I opened the door slightly and peered out, trying to catch a glimpse of the monster, when I saw a figure step out of a nearby building, his back toward me, as he began shouting at several soldiers who joined him.

"Kill the wolf," he said and pointed off toward where I knew Thomas and Alan would be. "Use those silver blades I gave you."

The half dozen soldiers nodded and ran off to follow orders, as the man turned, giving me a view of his face. Mordred looked directly at the house I was hiding in. A flood of memories crashed into my mind. Memories of Mordred attacking my friend and king,

Arthur. The memory of us fighting in France and me forced to choose between ending his life or saving Ivy's. Of me being unable to do either. It was at that point that I lost my temper.

CHAPTER 10

The front of the house exploded outward shooting brick and wood everywhere. Nearby properties were instantly demolished by the force.

"Mordred!" I roared as I darted toward him through the plume of smoke and dust I'd created.

I sent a ram of hardened air smashing into him, but he'd hastily created a shield of his own, pushing my magic aside and sending it crashing into a nearby building.

The move protected him from my magic, but it left him wide open to a physical attack. I ran at him, picking him up off his feet and dumping him head-first on the stone-littered ground.

I kicked him in the face as he tried to roll away, but he grabbed my leg and dragged me over him, pulling me off balance and using his own air magic to blast me in the chest, sending me flying back against a stone wall. For a moment, I lost the ability to take a breathe and watched in horror as Mordred used the time to gather his senses and run toward the boats I'd seen docked nearby.

I was about to give chase when a soldier emerged from a nearby house and raised his bow, aiming toward Thomas. I ignored Mordred, he would wait, he always did, and ran toward the archer. He saw me coming at the last minute and swung the bow toward me instead, letting me see the arrow clearly for the first time. Silver.

With the distance between us closed, I used a blade of fire to cleave through the wooden bow and string, before burying it in the archer's throat. I caught the arrow as it fell from his lifeless fingers and, after placing it in my belt, glanced over at Thomas, who was fending off the last of the soldiers with ease. I left my friend to his task and ran after Mordred who stood at the very end of a small wooden pier, looking out to the ocean beyond.

"No more running, Mordred," I said, and he turned to face me.

"You'll notice I wasn't running. I was waiting for you. I wanted you to know that those boys are already on that ship. They're going to die before they reach France. As will anyone else unfortunate enough to be aboard with them."

"Why? What do you want from all this? The boys aren't in line to the throne anymore."

"I promised Merlin that there would never be another of Arthur's blood to sit on the throne of England. I keep my promises."

"They were renounced," I told him again. "They will never sit on the throne."

"Merlin takes my threats seriously, I see."

I shook my head. "All of Arthur's descendants are removed from any kind of life in royalty."

"Yet, their mother was allowed to marry a king and create them. I plan on ending them. Arthur's line will never see power."

"That's why Richard is king, that's why they were renounced as soon as possible."

"Not quickly enough to stop one of them being made king!" Mordred screamed.

There clearly was no use arguing with Mordred about the princes. He'd sworn that none of Arthur's kin would rule after he'd attacked Arthur centuries earlier. Merlin had always been careful to keep Arthur's bloodline safe, but Mordred's threat had given him extra incentive. For some reason Merlin had neglected to hide the boys when they were born, maybe feeling that enough time had passed, or waiting to see what happened. Either way, Avalon was too slow and one of them had been crowned.

"I'm going to take them away from here," I told Mordred. "I'd prefer to go through you to get to them."

Mordred smiled. "A re-match already."

"Where's Ivy?" I demanded.

"The psychic girl?" He placed a finger to his temple. "You know, I often forget where I put her. She's quite easy to misplace."

"You will tell me everything I need to know," I promised.

"We'll see, 'old friend'."

I threw a plume of fire at Mordred, who responded by creating another shield of air and diverting the flame into the sea beneath us.

"Do you really think that magic is going to beat me?"

"Your choice," I said and sprinted forward.

He launched a kick where he thought my head would be, but I'd already stepped aside, grabbing his trousers with one hand and dragging him off balance, punching him in the jaw as he fell.

Mordred's head snapped aside, but he regained his balance more quickly than I'd expected and caught me in the knee with his foot. All my weight crashed down on a no longer usable limb, and I dropped to the wooden pier, landing on my knees with a crack. Mordred continued the attack, slamming his foot into the side of my head, knocking me down and then stamping on my ribs.

I rolled aside, catching a stinging blow to my elbow and

kicked out at Mordred's knee, but he stepped back, putting distance between us.

I got back to my feet, blood dripping slowly from my nose. "You need to try harder," I said.

"You're the one bleeding," Mordred pointed out. He quickly stepped forward and feinted with a kick, before trying to catch me in the head with a vicious elbow. Fortunately I saw it coming and blocked it, slamming my own elbow into his nose, which crunched from the force of the blow.

Mordred staggered back slightly, before snapping forward, his hand covered in dark glyphs as his blood magic activated. He tried to touch me, but I stepped back and drove the arrow I'd been holding into his forearm, causing his concentration to vanish, along with the blood magic he was wielding.

I kicked Mordred in the chest as hard as I could, sending him flailing back across the pier. He tried to scramble away, but I wrapped tendrils of air around his legs and pulled back with everything I had. Mordred flew across the pier, colliding with one of the docked boats, where I held him in place, hardening the air wrapped around him, as I stalked closer.

"That silver is making it difficult to use your magic," I said. "You should practice more with normal magic and less with your blood magic."

He reached over to the arrow and wrapped his fingers around it as I reached him. "Are you going to pull it out?" I asked. "Here let me help."

I tore the arrow from his forearm and then plunged it into the side of his knee, making him scream.

"Where's Ivy?" I asked. "You escaped with her in France, it won't happen again."

"Fuck you, Nathaniel. Fuck you and Avalon and Merlin and anyone else who thinks they can tell me what to do."

I was about to say something when a huge crash came from the ocean, and I turned to see a massive creature emerge from the depths near the now visible ship. Its appearance was close to that of a giant reptile. It was sixty or seventy feet long with a massive head and a mouth that could easily swallow a man whole. Its roar reverberated as if I were standing next to it, which, I was certain, would have been the worst place on earth to be. A massive tail whipped across the ocean causing huge waves and it swiped the air with its long arms, each one tipped with a massive claw half as tall as a man. It roared once again and smashed its arm down on the bow of the ship.

"Leviathan," I whispered and heard the shock in my voice. I knew Alan was powerful, and touched in the head, but I hadn't thought he was powerful or crazy enough to summon one of the true giants of the ocean.

My attention had turned away for just over a second, maybe two, but it was enough. I turned back to Mordred as he sprung to his feet and plunged a dagger of blood magic just under my ribs. I forgot how to breathe, stumbling back as pain exploded all over my body. It forced me away from Mordred and I crashed onto the pier. He smiled and showed me the blade of blood magic that he'd created in his hand. A second later the expression changed to one of shock as he coughed up blood and immediately slumped to his knees. I raised my hand to show Mordred the blade of air, covered in his blood, which stretched out from the back of my hand.

I removed the blade and placed a hand to my ribs, igniting my fire magic, searing the flesh to stop the bleeding. I screamed out in pain.

Mordred laughed and coughed up more blood. "You know I'll live though, yes?"

"Yes, but I also know it hurts like hell. I'll take the little moments of happiness when I can get them."

"I really do fucking hate you, you know that."

"It's come up before," I pointed out.

"Your summoner friend is insane for bringing a leviathan here. There aren't many of them left. They're as rare as dragons."

I couldn't disagree with him.

"It's tearing that French ship apart. There are blood magic curse marks on the timber, I can feel them being torn apart."

"The marks or the people?"

Mordred was silent for a second. "Both. Their blood washes over my marks."

I glanced over at the monster which was tearing into the ship as if it were made of nothing more than straw. It grabbed something in its massive hand, raised it to its maw and dropped it in. "Soldiers," I said. "They shouldn't be here in the first place."

"Ah, no sympathy for the enemy, is that how it is, Nathaniel?"

"If Alan hadn't summoned a leviathan, they would have died at your hands anyway. I assume your way would have been much less pleasant."

"Than being eaten alive?" Mordred looked thoughtful for a second. "Yes, my way would have hurt much more."

We sat in silence for a short time. Neither of us able to do anything but bleed and hurt. It was probably the first time in eight hundred years we weren't trying to kill each other for being in such close proximity. If you didn't count the fact that we had been at each others throats a few minutes earlier, anyway.

"What are you going to do, Mordred?" I asked. "When those princes are safe, are you still going to try to kill them, or are you going to run away?"

Mordred continued to watch the leviathan destroy the French ship and crew and didn't answer. But a short time later the monster vanished back under the waves with a colossal wave that magically dissipated. A substantially smaller wave rushed over the end of the pier. When it was gone, two young boys stood, wet and scared. A smaller version of the leviathan stood behind them. It nodded to me and then dove back into the ocean. The two princes had been delivered to the pier by a young leviathan. Alan's power astonished me, but my thoughts quickly turned to Mordred, who was watching the two princes like a wolf watches a farmer's sheep.

"You know what you asked me earlier?" Mordred said. "I can do both."

He sprang to his feet and darted forward, but I managed to get in front of him, blocking his path several feet short of the princes and driving a blade of fire into his stomach. "Now this *is* going to hurt," I whispered and tore the dagger out of him, turning it into a whip of fire as it moved, almost cleaving Mordred horizontally in half.

He dropped to his knees and tried to hold his insides in as his blood quickly drenched both himself and the pier. Blood magic glyphs lit up over his arms and while part of me wanted to finish the job, to stop whatever healing he was trying to perform, I had more important matters. Mordred wasn't going anywhere until he'd managed to heal himself.

I turned to the two boys. The youngest, Richard, was scared and tired looking, while his older brother, Edward, wore a look of defiance.

"Who are you?" Edward demanded.

"Nathaniel Garrett," I told him. "I'm here to take you to safety."

"Buckingham lied to me and took us by force. He was going to kill us to start a war."

"I know," I said. "Was he on the ship?"

Edward shook his head. "He left to go alone several days ago.

What was it that attacked the ship and brought us here?"

I saw no reason to hide the truth. "A leviathan. They're intelligent creatures, more related to dragons. It would be best if you didn't mention them ever again."

"A dragon saved me from a ship and its child brought me and my brother to shore inside a wave." Edward chuckled, but there was no humor in it. "I don't believe I'll be mentioning it to anyone."

He glanced behind me at Mordred. "Did you hurt him?" Edward's eyes hardened, and I wondered what Mordred had done during his time holding the boys captive.

I nodded.

"Can we leave now?" Richard asked softly.

"Yes, we'll take you to Brighton for a few days; you can rest up until Avalon arrives to take you to safety."

"Avalon. I was told about them before I took the crown," Edward said. "I assume I won't be returning to my kingship."

"No, you'll be taken somewhere safe to live out your lives in whatever matter you see fit. You'll live good, long, happy lives, but you will never rule anyone."

"And our mother?"

"She'll be informed that you're safe and well," I explained. "And she'll be able to come see you both when you're settled."

I led the boys off the pier, meeting Thomas who was bloody, but in human form. "We won then," he said.

"Something along those lines, yes," I told him. "Take Edward and Richard somewhere safe in the village; I'll go finish with Mordred."

"Enjoy," Thomas said and signaled the two boys to follow him.

I watched them walk off and then slowly made my way back to Mordred, who was leaning up against another wooden post near the end of the pier.

"So, you're going to kill me?" he called out.

"Yes, Mordred. I'm going to end you once and for all. But first, I'm going to make you tell me where Ivy is."

I was about ten feet from him when the ocean exploded up around the end of the pier and the young leviathan leapt onto the wooden boards next to Mordred, grabbing the injured man and dragging him into the waves before I could stop him.

"Alan," I screamed. "You bastard."

Alan appeared just beside the pier, his entire body made of the same water he stood upon.

"I'll kill you for this," I said.

"Sorry, Nathaniel, but you never mentioned that it was Mordred you were going up against. If you had, I'd have never joined you. I owe Mordred, and, quite frankly, I'm a lot more scared of him than I am of you." With that he vanished back into the waves, leaving me raging and bloody on the pier.

EPILOGUE

It took weeks to get the boys settled in at Avalon and to sort out the mess that Mordred and Buckingham had created. The entire contents of Alan's house had vanished, although he left the crowns behind, which I melted down to nothing when I burned his home to the ground.

By the time I got around to getting back to London, Richard had executed Buckingham and then been killed in the battle at Bosworth Field. Merlin explained that he'd allowed Richard to die, since Henry, who had just been crowned, was a better long-term prospect. Even so, I requested that I be the one to give the new king his welcome to the world he now found himself in.

Unfortunately for Henry, I'd begun to hear fabricated tales of Richard's wickedness and cowardice well before I'd reached London. By the time I found myself actually walking into the Tower of London, the tales turned from fantasy to reality. They included Richard's naked body being paraded through the city and his grave site being whatever river they'd dumped his body into.

The celebration that was being held in the king's court when I arrived only hardened the anger I was feeling at the treatment of someone I'd respected.

I walked through the crowd of people, who were all enjoying

themselves to the sounds of the lute and harp, and stopped before Henry.

"Do you not bow before your king, knave?" an older woman beside Henry asked.

"My name is Hellequin," I allowed my air magic to carry the word around the court. Enough people there knew of Avalon, and it didn't take long for them to quiet others. Once silence had descended, I continued without looking back at the crowd. "Anyone who isn't I or the king leave. Now."

The entire room emptied apart from me, the king and the older woman.

"How dare you speak to my son in this manner," the older woman snapped.

I waved my hand and she fell silent, the air removed from her lungs. She choked and coughed and dropped to her knees.

"If you speak to me in that way again, I will burst the lungs in your chest," I informed her before allowing her to breathe again.

"Black magic, demon… demon spawn," she stuttered, remaining on the floor.

"It's magic, but nothing black about it," I assured her without taking my gaze off Henry, who was the very picture of shock. "I come from Avalon. I assume you have been told about us."

Henry nodded. "I am king because you allow it," he said. "Does that sum it up?"

"That's a pretty good summation, yes."

"I don't understand why you're so angry, though. I won the battle against Richard fair and square."

"Less than fair," I said. "But I don't begrudge you a win. I begrudge your treatment of Richard after his death."

"He was not fit to be king. He was without God's will," the older woman said.

"Your name is Margaret, is it not?" I asked her and she nodded. "As you're the king's mother, I will give you one final warning. Be silent or leave."

She opened her mouth to speak, but Henry raised his hand and she remained silent. "Do not speak to her in that way," he said calmly. "Your anger is with me."

He had a point and I took a deep breath. "Richard doesn't deserve the lies of cowardice and rumors that he had his nephews murdered. Neither of those things is true. He was a good man."

"I agree," Henry said to my utter shock. "But whatever I think, the damage is already done. I cannot recant a rumor any more than I can turn the tides away from the shore."

"You can bury him properly though."

"Yes, overzealous followers are wont to do stupid things. His body is already being recovered and will be buried. There will be no fanfare or procession for his legacy, but I will not allow him to be dumped in the river like rubbish. Does this ease your anger?"

"I liked him," I said louder than I'd meant to. "You killed someone I liked, and I should take your head for it. I've killed for less. But you are needed here."

Henry remained silent for a short time. "He was not a bad man," he finally said. "But I defeated him, and I am now king. My destiny was always to wear the crown and rule this land. I do not take my responsibilities lightly."

To be honest the meeting wasn't going the way I'd expected. I'd hoped he would be so full of pomp and arrogance that I could vent and make him fear me with satisfaction. But instead, he was calm and rational, making me seem to be the crazy asshole who'd stormed a king's coronation.

"You will be the best king this land can have," I told him.

"You will bring stability and common-sense to these people. Because anything less and Avalon will send someone for a second visit, and they're normally a lot less pleasant than the first."

Henry stepped forward and placed a hand on my shoulder. "I am sorry that I am not the king you wanted. But I will be the king these people need. I *will* do great things and I will not dishonor this crown or position."

I looked him in the eyes as he spoke. His mother would try to control him. I'd heard she'd been trying to arrange power for her son for many years, and I doubted she would stop just because he'd achieved her goal. If Henry could become his own man, he could be a great king.

We spoke for a short time more about what Avalon wished of him, and I left believing that maybe England could gain some stability after so many years of civil wars. As I exited the Tower of London, I said a silent good-bye to Richard and hoped that at some point people would remember him for his bravery in battle and his willingness to try to create peace in the country he lived. And not as the monster the tales were beginning to suggest.

ACKNOWLEDGEMENT

The list of people I need to thank for helping me put this novella out is no shorter than when producing a full-length novel.

Firstly, my wife and 3 daughters. You are, and always shall be, one of the main reasons I write. Your unwavering support and interest in what I do, makes those long days of editing and pulling my hair out over a tiny plot decision worthwhile. I love you all.

My parents, the rest of my friends and family, you too have always supported me and I probably wouldn't be here right now, typing out these words without it. Thank you.

To D.B.Reynolds and Michelle Muto, both incredible writers and friends and both deserving of every accolade and fan they receive. Never could I have hoped to meet two more amazing people.

To my editors, Jennifer Gaynor and Bea, you both helped create this novella with your red pen and suggestions. You both have my eternal gratude for your help.

Eamon O'Donoghue. The man who has done my covers since Crimes Against Magic was published over 18 months ago (seriously where has the time gone?) I'm honored that you agree to do the covers for me. I probably owe you several pints of beer by now.

To everyone on Facebook or Twitter who took the time to say hi and tell me they enjoyed the books. To those of you who e-mailed and did the same, or spent a few minutes writing a review. Thank you. It's always a pleasure to get feedback and be able to talk to people who are as excited about my work as I am.

ABOUT THE AUTHOR

Steve McHugh is an Award nominated, bestselling fantasy author. 13 books published and counting. Father of 3 daughters. Owner of epic backlog of videogames.

Blog: https://stevejmchugh.wordpress.com/

Twitter: https://twitter.com/StevejMchugh

Facebook: https://www.facebook.com/steveJMchugh

Amazon: https://amzn.to/2BYLi72

Printed in Great Britain
by Amazon